To Ride a Butterfly

Illustration by John Wallner

To Ride a Butterfly

Original Pictures, Stories, Poems, & Songs for Children

By Fifty-two Distinguished Authors and Illustrators

Edited by Nancy Larrick and Wendy Lamb

WITH A LETTER FROM BARBARA BUSH

In Celebration of the Twenty-fifth Anniversary of

READING IS FUNDAMENTAL®

BANTAM DOUBLEDAY DELL

Published by
Bantam Doubleday Dell Publishing Group, Inc.
666 Fifth Avenue
New York, New York 10103

Reading Is Fundamental, RIF, and the unique design showing an open
book with a smiling face on it and Reading Is Fundamental underneath
are all registered service marks of Reading Is Fundamental, Inc.,
and are used with permission. All rights reserved.

This book was set in Palatino and Optima Medium.

Library of Congress Cataloging-in-Publication Data
To ride a butterfly : new pictures, stories, folktales, fables,
nonfiction, poems, and songs for young children / by 52 outstanding
American authors and illustrators of books for young children ;
edited by Nancy Larrick and Wendy Lamb ; with a letter from Barbara Bush.
        p.   cm.
"Celebrating the 25th anniversary of the founding of Reading is Fundamental."
Includes bibliographical references and index.
Summary: An illustrated collection of fables, folktales, stories,
poems, songs, and nonfiction by a variety of authors and illustrators.
ISBN 0-440-50402-3
1. Children's literature, American.   [1. Literature—Collections.]
I. Larrick, Nancy. II. Lamb, Wendy. III. Reading is Fundamental, inc.
        PZ5.T457   1991   810.8'09282—dc20
                91-7778   CIP   AC
Manufactured in the United States of America.

October 1991

10 9 8 7 6 5 4 3 2 1

LBM

The following authors and artists have given their time and talents to create this book. All royalties from this book will go to Reading Is Fundamental.

Verna Aardema	Bill Martin Jr.
Aliki	Petra Mathers
John Archambault	Eve Merriam
Franklyn M. Branley	Else Holmelund Minarik
Natalie Savage Carlson	Lilian Moore
Lucille Clifton	Lillian Morrison
Barbara Cohen	Brian Pinkney
Tomie dePaola	Patricia Polacco
Beatrice Schenk de Regniers	Deborah Kogan Ray
Aileen Fisher	Ken Robbins
Patricia Reilly Giff	Anne Rockwell
Andrew Glass	Glen Rounds
Tom Glazer	Cynthia Rylant
Karen Gundersheimer	Seymour Simon
Will Hillenbrand	Blanche Sims
Lillian Hoban	Peter Spier
Mary Ann Hoberman	Robin Spowart
Nonny Hogrogian	John Steptoe
Patricia Hubbell	Tomi Ungerer
David Kherdian	Neil Waldman
Robert Kraus	John Wallner
Karla Kuskin	Rosemary Wells
Madeleine L'Engle	Nancy Willard
Emily Arnold McCully	Taro Yashima
Ann McGovern	Jane Yolen
Patricia C. McKissack	Charlotte Zolotow

To Ride a Butterfly was designed by Kathleen Westray

MANY OTHERS HELPED TO CREATE THIS BOOK:

At Bantam Doubleday Dell:

Doris Bass, *overall direction*
George Nicholson and Betsy Gould, *editorial support*
Lou Bilka, Rusty Hannon, Joe Gannon, and Richard Derus, *production*
Johanna Tani and Karen Prince, *copyediting*
Dorothy Boyajy, *contracts*
Suzanne Telsey, *legal advice*
Liza Wright, *publicity*

THESE COMPANIES GENEROUSLY DONATED THEIR SERVICES:

Text paper is Patina Matte by S.D. WARREN COMPANY, a subsidiary of
SCOTT PAPER COMPANY
Printed and bound by LAKE BOOK MANUFACTURING, INC., Melrose Park, Ill.
Separations provided by NEW INTERLITHO S.p.A., Milan, Italy
Stripping and filmwork by R.R. DONNELLEY & SONS, Crawfordsville, Ind.
Additional filmwork by AUTHENTICOLOR, New York, N.Y.
Typesetting supplied by PAGESETTERS, INC., Brattleboro, Vt.
Cover filmwork and printing by MIKEN SYSTEMS, INC., Cheektowaga, N.Y.
Endpapers supplied by ECOLOGICAL FIBERS, INC., Lunenberg, Mass.
Jacket printing by FOUR SEASONS LITHO, Plainview, N.Y.
Jacket paper supplied by WESTVACO, New York, N.Y.
Cartons supplied by ROYAL CONTINENTAL BOX COMPANY, Cicero, Ill.
Binders board supplied by the DAVEY COMPANY.

To Ride a Butterfly

Don't be like the two caterpillars who were
crawling along on the ground when a butterfly flew
over them. And one caterpillar said to the other,
"You'll never catch me going up on one of those."
But I'll ride a butterfly any day.
And I hope you will too.

—MADELEINE L'ENGLE

*From her Smith College commencement address
entitled "To Ride a Butterfly"*

THE WHITE HOUSE

January 14, 1991

Dear Friends,

What a wonderfully appropriate coincidence that 1991, the Year of the Lifetime Reader, is the year that Reading Is Fundamental (RIF) is celebrating its 25th anniversary. RIF is dedicated to helping today's children grow up to be lifetime readers, and to getting the whole family involved in the process.

This beautiful anthology was created for RIF's 25th birthday and will help more children and families deepen their love of reading.

Reading has always been one of my greatest pleasures—alone, with my children when they were younger, and now with my grandchildren. No matter what age reader *you* are, you can share in bringing stories like these to life for others.

I wholeheartedly encourage you to read to and with others in your family. It can be one of life's most rewarding experiences, and there is no better way to create lifelong readers.

Warmly,

Barbara Bush

"Reading & Riding" by seven-year-old Kimberly Connett
of Noblesville, Indiana, winner of the RIF National Poster Contest

That All May Read

TWENTY-FIVE years ago Reading Is Fundamental (RIF) began as a small program with a single premise: that reading is an essential part of childhood and that all children need and deserve to have appealing books of their own. RIF has now brought more than 100 million free books to American children—books they chose to take home, to keep, to read, and to love. For many, these are the only books they will have of their own.

Today's new generation of RIF children reflects the rich mosaic of American childhood experience, coming as they do from isolated Alaskan villages and crowded major cities; from the multiethnic neighborhoods of the Southwest; from remote rural areas and two-hundred-year-old Appalachian communities.

All of these children can revel in the beauty, the excitement, the enrichment that comes from reading and books. They can discover that reading is a bridge to new friends, new experiences, and new worlds. Opening a book for the first time, reading a bedtime story with a family member, swapping favorite books with friends are all treasured joys of childhood. When we introduce our children to books, we give them the opportunity to blossom in mind and spirit.

To Ride a Butterfly is a collection of poems, stories, songs, drawings, and paintings contributed by distinguished writers and illustrators who themselves believe that "reading is fundamental."

A true literary celebration of childhood, this anthology is the result of an extraordinary collaboration of talent and resources. RIF is grateful to the hundreds of people who have made it possible.

In particular, we salute the Bantam Doubleday Dell Publishing Group for undertaking this unique cooperative venture for the benefit of Reading Is Fundamental and the millions of children we reach.

In addition, we wish to thank Nancy Larrick for her leadership in bringing together these literary and artistic contributions and her thoughtful editing of the whole.

Finally, we wish to thank each of the fifty-two writers and artists whose creations make *To Ride a Butterfly* a treasure to be enjoyed for years to come.

We welcome you and the children you love to this remarkable book and invite each of you to let your imagination take flight on its wings.

MRS. ELLIOT RICHARDSON
Chairman of the Board

RUTH GRAVES, President
READING IS FUNDAMENTAL, INC.

Reading Is Fundamental, Inc. (RIF) is a nationwide nonprofit organization that works for literacy by helping America's young people grow up reading. With reading motivation activities, books to own, outreach to parents and communities, and public education, RIF works to create a climate in homes, schools, communities, and the nation that supports and encourages children's reading. Since 1966 RIF has gotten more than one hundred million books into the hands and homes—and futures—of American children.

Reading Is Fundamental, Inc.
Smithsonian Institution
600 Maryland Ave., S.W., Suite 500
Washington, D.C. 20560

At Home and at School

Let's look at the pictures. . . .
Let's read the story. . . .
Now let's talk about it. . . .
Then . . . *let's do it again!*

THIS is what we hear from children who have come under the spell of stories and poems by outstanding writers and illustrations by renowned artists.

These are children who have been drawn into listening to stories read aloud, searching the pictures, chanting the poems, and then reading on their own with delight.

To Ride a Butterfly is an original collection of stories, poems, and songs, written and illustrated for young children: those just on the verge of learning to read, those venturing boldly on their own, and those probing the how and why of everything around them. These children are in what have been called "the peak language-learning years." This is when they learn to listen, to talk, to read, and to write—all language arts they must count on throughout their lives. How well they develop these skills and use them will depend in large measure on their mentors at home—parents, of course, but also those who substi-

tute as parents: grandparents, older siblings, and baby-sitters.

At school the teacher must build on the experiences the child has had at home. Again and again I have had teachers tell me, "I can always spot the child who is read to at home. He talks comfortably, he has a sense of story, and he is eager to read on his own."

Innumerable research studies have come to the same conclusion: children who have been read to on a regular basis are the ones who become good readers and continue to reach out for more. These are the ones ready "to ride a butterfly."

I wish every child could be part of a daily read-aloud session at home as well as at school. It may be for only ten or fifteen minutes, but it should be every day and should be thought of as the time for fun, for delight—no quizzing or scolding, no blaming or pouting. This is the time for sheer pleasure—uninterrupted pleasure, I might add.

That means turning off radio and TV, closing the door on distractions, and unwinding for peaceful comradeship.

Often the read-aloud session can successfully include children of different ages—the older ones hearing their old favorites and sometimes reading aloud to the little ones. Both age levels gain from such shared experience.

To keep to a daily schedule it may help to set aside the same time every day for reading aloud—after lunch for the preschooler, perhaps, just after supper or at bedtime for the older ones.

The more children become involved in such read-aloud sessions, the more they seem to enjoy it. One way to draw the younger ones in at first is to help them look for details in the pictures. For example, note the books that make the bridge in Peter Spier's watercolor on pages 26–27, the ducks and geese in the river, the birds overhead, and, as one first grader reminded me, "Don't forget the dragonflies!"

Certainly when you read Nancy Willard's poem, page 17, you will want to give the child the fun of looking for the "magic horses" in Emily McCully's painting opposite.

Looking is only part of it. Children like to chime in on the sound of language as well. Note the repeated lines of "Saturday Night at the Fair," by Bill Martin Jr. and John Archambault. You can almost croon the lines, you know—made even more fun if you chant one line and your young partner chants the next.

Both of the songs in *To Ride a Butterfly*—"You Are," by Tom Glazer, and "Little Red Hen," by Mary Ann Hoberman—invite immediate involvement. Tom Glazer gives suggestions for "performing" his song, as he puts it. And the repetition in "Little Red Hen" is an invitation to chime in.

The stories in *To Ride a Butterfly* range from the simple picture stories with words ("One Plus One," by Aliki, and "Spider Learns to Read," by Robert Kraus) to folktales and longer stories such as those by Patricia C. McKissack, John Steptoe, Ann McGovern, Patricia Reilly Giff, and Anne Rockwell. All of these, and many more, furnish the opportunity for the child to take part—talking about the pictures and the situations, then retelling the picture stories of Aliki and Robert Kraus. The longer stories invite questioning and pondering, rereading, and further conversation. And, more than any story in the book, "Soapy Smith, the Boastful Cowboy, or The Skunk in the Bunkhouse" will bring giggles and more giggles.

Several pieces in *To Ride a Butterfly* are nonfiction—including "Orion, the Great Hunter," by Franklyn M. Branley, and "The Magnificent Voyager," by Seymour Simon. Both will appeal to children of the Space Age. Both can lead to further questioning as well as reading about the exploration of outer space and perhaps examining maps and charts of the sky.

"Tell Me Again!" and "My Grandmother's Hair" are reminiscences. Else Holmelund Minarik recalls a dramatic incident when she was only four, growing up in Denmark. Cynthia Rylant writes of a childhood experience with her grandmother in West Virginia. Possibly each of these could lead to talk about childhood experiences never to be forgotten, or to an interview with grandparents who might be drawn into reminiscences of their own.

And throughout the book there are poems —amusing, charming, and always singing.

We hope that this rich array of literature and art will win the hearts of young listeners and readers so that they will grow up with a sense of humor and a sense of wonder, ready to "ride a butterfly any day."

NANCY LARRICK
Editor

CONTENTS

MY MOTHER'S MAGIC EYES INVENT HORSES

By Nancy Willard
Illustrated by Emily Arnold McCully

My mother's magic eyes invent horses.
When she looks out the window she says,
"See the two green horses in the garden?"

My eyes aren't magic. I see two green bushes
leaning together, the best of friends.
I say, "Put on your glasses, Mother."

She puts on her glasses. No horses.
She says the bushes have swallowed them.
Bushes are careless and horses are shy.

One day I covered my eyes and called,
"Horses, horses, come to me."
Something licked my hand—was it rain?

Something brushed my ear—was it wind?
Something said, "We are two green friends,
leaning together, the best of horses."

I opened my eyes.
I saw two horses,
green as clover and tall as my knees.

Then seven dogs ran into the garden.
Seven dogs chasing two green horses!
I said, "Put on your glasses, Mother,

quick!"
She put on her glasses,
just in time.

SATURDAY NIGHT AT THE FAIR

**By Bill Martin Jr.
and John Archambault
Illustrated by Lillian Hoban**

We're dancing,
We're prancing,
We're simply
romancing,
Saturday night at the fair,

We're whirling,
We're twirling,
our dreams
are unfurling,
Saturday night at the fair,

Mama and Papa and all of us kids,
strolling along hand in hand,
Hot dogs and popcorn
and sweet cotton candy
spun to the beat of the band. . . .

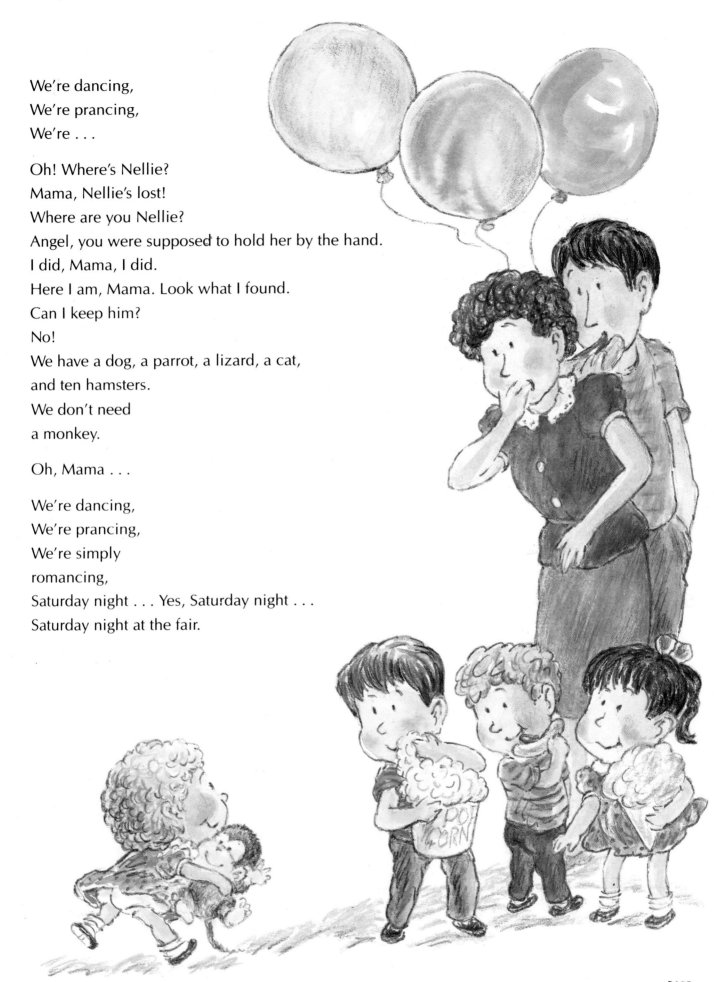

We're dancing,
We're prancing,
We're . . .

Oh! Where's Nellie?
Mama, Nellie's lost!
Where are you Nellie?
Angel, you were supposed to hold her by the hand.
I did, Mama, I did.
Here I am, Mama. Look what I found.
Can I keep him?
No!
We have a dog, a parrot, a lizard, a cat,
and ten hamsters.
We don't need
a monkey.

Oh, Mama . . .

We're dancing,
We're prancing,
We're simply
romancing,
Saturday night . . . Yes, Saturday night . . .
Saturday night at the fair.

THE CAT WHO WENT TO THE CASTLE

By Anne Rockwell • Illustrated by Petra Mathers

A POOR family once lived on a small farm at the edge of a great forest. Although they were poor they were very happy. They had a spotted cow that gave good milk for cheese. They sold their cheese in the market on the other side of the forest. They had a cat who kept the mice from eating the cheese and who purred their little girl to sleep every night. They had everything they wanted.

All went well for them until one day wild onions sprouted in the meadow where the spotted cow grazed each day. The cow's milk tasted like onions and so did the cheese. No one would buy it, and before long the family had no money for food.

"I will sell my sharp knife," said the father, and he did.

But soon this money was spent and wild onions still grew in the meadow.

"I will sell my beautiful red and gold kerchief," said the mother, and she did. But soon this money, too, was spent and the family went hungry.

Near the town where the market was held each Wednesday there stood a great stone castle. The countess who ruled the castle had a cat that she loved so much, it was never allowed to lift a paw. Her cat, who was called Lord Pussetty, lay on a velvet cushion, day and night. He drank sweet cream and ate shiny sardines from gold and silver bowls. While the big, fat, spoiled cat got fatter and lazier, rats and mice overran the castle.

At last the countess decided something must be done. She would buy another cat, but this cat would have to work hard.

A sign went up on the castle gates:

WANTED: GOOD MOUSER.
PRICE: TWO PIECES OF SILVER.

The poor family soon read this sign.

"Will we have to sell our cat?" asked the little girl. She began to cry, for she already knew the answer.

Her father said, "No! No! I will sell my ax instead."

But his wife said, "Then how will we keep warm when winter comes? Without your ax you cannot chop wood, and without firewood we will all freeze to death."

And the man knew his wife was right. The little girl knew it too.

On Wednesday, when the market came to town, she put the little cat in a basket and walked sadly up to the castle.

The countess looked at the cat scornfully.

"She is a good mouser," said the little girl.

"Well, I will give you one piece of silver for that puny-looking cat," said the countess.

Before the little girl could remind her that she had offered two pieces of silver, a servant gave her one small silver coin. Then he pushed her out the gates and across the drawbridge.

The cat was set to work, and work she did. All night she chased mice while Lord Pussetty slept on his soft velvet cushion. In the morning when the exhausted little cat meowed for something tasty to eat and drink, the countess threw a shoe at her. Lord Pussetty lapped his sweet cream and nibbled his shiny sardines out of his gold and silver bowls. Then he licked his paws and

Lord Pussetty every time she even came near his velvet cushion and his gold and silver bowls. And she certainly did not like the countess.

One day this little cat decided she had had enough. When a rat ventured across the floor she did not even twitch a whisker. Instead, she yawned and stretched and lazily began to wash her face.

"Catch that rat, you wicked creature!" screamed the countess.

But the little cat did not move an inch. Instead, she meowed loudly to the countess. Only Lord Pussetty could understand what she was saying, and this is what he heard:

"You bought me for one small silver coin and I have already caught more than thirty mice and three big rats! You have screamed at me and thrown things at me and given me nothing to eat or drink. I will serve you no more!"

All that is what the little cat said, but only Lord Pussetty understood.

The next day was Wednesday, the day the market was held. A servant opened the gates of the castle that afternoon so some market carts could enter the courtyard. The cart wheels made such a clatter that no one noticed when the little cat slipped out through the open gates. She ran across the drawbridge and down the road to the town.

But the little cat did not find her family at the market that Wednesday. They had no reason to come, for they had no cheese to sell and no money to buy anything.

So the little cat had to set off for home all by herself.

Between the market and home lay the dark forest. Just as the little cat reached it, the sun went down. Soon the moon and

washed his whiskers and smirked at the little working cat.

Days and nights passed at the castle. The little cat caught so many mice that soon only big rats were left. She began catching them. But still the countess never rewarded her with something tasty to eat or drink and a comfortable cushion to sleep on. The cat lived on what she caught and drank water from the fountain where the servants washed the pots and pans. She did not like the taste of rats and mice, and soon she became as thin as Lord Pussetty was fat.

She was very sad. She missed her family. She missed the father and mother, but most of all she missed the little girl. And she did not like being hissed at and scratched at by stars came out to light the sky, but the cat could not see them through the tops of the tall trees.

Suddenly an owl hooted. The little cat hid quickly beneath a thorny bush. Thorns scratched her but she did not come out until she saw the huge owl swoop down past her and fly away through the woods.

Then the little cat tiptoed silently on her way through the dark forest. She was so frightened that the fur on her back stood straight up.

A wolf began to howl, and the little cat knew it was not far away. She ran up a tall tree to hide, and just in time. Right below her she could make out the wolf's big gray shape running through the forest.

From her perch high in the tree she could see the moon and stars shining far above the dark forest. But one small star seemed to have fallen to Earth, for it flickered near the edge of the horizon, just beyond the forest.

Suddenly the little cat scrambled joyfully down the tree trunk. She knew that what she saw was not a fallen star. Instead, it was a light that shone from the window of her very own home!

She ran and ran until she was out of the dark forest. Before long she was racing through the meadow where the spotted cow grazed each day. And then she was home. She scratched at the door.

"Do you hear something?" asked the father.

The little cat meowed.

"Only the wind wailing," said the mother.

"Shhhh!" said the little girl. She listened carefully. The cat meowed and scratched at the door again, louder this time.

"I know what that is!" the little girl cried. She ran and opened the door.

What did she see but her own dear little cat? She picked her up and kissed her and patted her fur and scratched her ears. Then she set out a saucer of milk for her. Even though it tasted of wild onions, the little cat thought it was delicious.

Everyone was happy to see the little cat again. And that very night the wild onions withered and died in the meadow. It seemed the little cat had brought good fortune home with her.

Soon there was good cheese to sell at the market again. No mice ate it—the little cat saw to that. Everything was just as it had been.

Except for one thing. Never, never would the little cat go to the market with her family again. It was just too close to the castle.

CAT POEMS

Written and illustrated by Karla Kuskin

Toots's Ears

Let us begin with Tootsie's ears
intelligent
on guard
alert
to any sound of mouse or bird.
A mouse or bird could be dessert.

Her Nose

There is no nose I know
no nose I think
no point as pale and pink,
a rose among fur snows.
If I could choose
to be a snoot as suitable
as it that sits on Toots
I would have chose
to be that very nose.

Her Tail

Following Toots like a boa or banner,
waving farewell in a marvelous manner,
smoke-gray and silky
a billowing sail
following Toots with a flourish:
her tail.

Cat at Rest

In the sun pool
like a curled fur shell you lie
breathing light purrs
inhaling the scene
through one green
half-open eye.

When our cat is at rest
our house is at rest
and so is the earth and sky.

. . . reading is your bridge

to a wonderful future!

—Peter Spier

A HAMSTER . . . BUT

By Aileen Fisher

My mother says a hamster
is an easy pet to keep:
it's furry and it's cuddly
in a golden little heap.
It doesn't need to scamper
down the street, and race and run,
so the leash law wouldn't hamper
such a pet from having fun.

My mother says a hamster
makes entertaining squeaks,
and grows two furry pockets
in its chubby little cheeks.
It stuffs them quite compactly
with food in bits and lumps
until it looks exactly
like a hamster with the mumps.

My mother says a hamster
needs very little space.
It wears a calm expression
on its neatly whiskered face.

It's gentle and it's cheerful
and just the sort of pet
a person who is tearful
over leashes ought to get.

But I'd rather,
really rather
please, I'd rather
have a *dog*.

ONE AND ONE

The Story of Two Eggs

Written and illustrated by Aliki

My hen laid an egg
as she did every day.

I pierced it and blew
all the insides away.

I painted the shell

and hung it with care.

Then scrambled the egg

for my breakfast with Bear.

The next time my hen
sat asleep on her straw

I waited around—
and then guess what I saw!

She stood as the egg shook

and started to crack.

Then out popped a chick!

So I gave it a snack.

LITTLE RED HEN

Words and Music by Mary Ann Hoberman
Illustrated by Robin Spowart

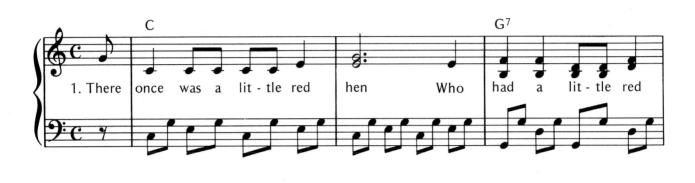

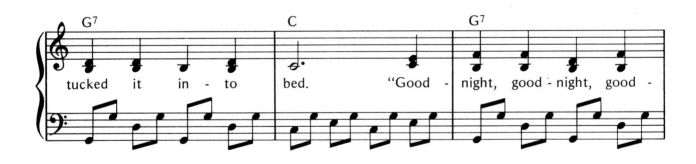

2) There once was a little red hen
   And she had a little red wing
   And every night in the pale moonlight
   She began to sing.

   　　　Good night, etc.

3) There once was a little red hen
   And she had a little red breast
   And every night in the pale moonlight
   She tucked it in her nest.

   　　　Good night, etc.

4) There once was a little brown hen, etc.

5) There once was a little white hen, etc.

6) There once was a little black hen, etc.

TERENCE TOAD AND THE VISITOR

By David Kherdian • Illustrated by Nonny Hogrogian

MY name is Terence and I am a toad. Terence Toad. I live in this old rock garden for the one and only reason that it is no longer cared for. If it was cared for, I wouldn't have any privacy. And privacy, as I like to say, is my middle name.

There is an English couple living near here. They have a son named Michael, who has taken a fancy to this little rock garden. He comes at least once a day to check on the toads—namely me. He's a friendly little chap, this Michael, with a loud, bubbly laugh. He not only doesn't mean any harm but has quite simply fallen in love with us little creatures.

It's our wee-bittyness that probably does it, since any one of us toads (at least), from the eldest to the youngest, would fit snugly and comfortably in his hand. But you see, he is so young, so easily excited, that he might just accidentally drop our little stone houses on our heads.

It's a custom with us to make our homes by burrowing a space under a stone. One toad to a stone, that's our motto. And of course, since we are agreed on this, it all works out pretty well.

For a long time Michael would come to my house and lift up my stone, look at me, chuckle, gurgle, and scream with delight. Then—and only then—he would put down my rock (almost perfectly where he found it) and go running for home.

This went on day after day and week after week until I got fed up with living in a goldfish bowl, as the saying is. So I decided I had no choice but to pack myself off in search of another home in a more secluded part of the garden.

Well, do you know what happened next? Michael just kept coming back, day after day, looking for me under my old stone house. Then, when he found that I was no longer there, he would sigh mournfully and go racing back home to his mom.

Little by little by little I started to take

pity on him because, to tell you the truth, if he had disappeared on me the way I had disappeared on him, I would have felt pretty low myself. What made it worse was that I went on seeing him every day, same as always, but he wasn't able to see me.

Well, just about the time I was considering moving back, here comes little Michael with a toy toad that he must have found in his play box, which he proceeded to stick under *my* old rock.

From that day on he came and visited his old fake toad every afternoon. I couldn't tell if he was pretending it was me, or if he'd forgotten me altogether and thought that his fake toad was for real, or what.

Anyhow, it was a good show, as the English say, and as far as I was concerned it was the best of two worlds: I got to see Michael every day and I got to see him *happy*. And my own life and privacy were no longer in danger.

But one day, here comes the frog Freddy into *my* garden. He instantly took up residence under a rock next to *my* old home. Well, you guessed it. It wasn't long before Michael (probably from waking up on the wrong side of his bed one morning) turned over the wrong rock and discovered old Freddy Frog. From that day on the fake toad was forgotten and upstart Freddy became the living scream of the garden.

So here I sit, forgotten and forlorn in my once peaceful but neglected garden. What I think I should do is this: make a new home next to the stone that is next to the stone my old home was next to. Then one day, when Michael wakes up on the wrong side of the bed, he'll turn my stone over and see me again.

The unpredictability of it appeals to me, as the certainty of *always* being seen didn't. And even if he doesn't ever find me, it will be bound to upset Freddy, and I will have a secret little game all my own.

HUFF AND PUFF

By Eve Merriam

To a little to,
fro a little fro,
stamp your heel
and away you go.

Kith a little kith,
kin a little kin,
choose your partner
and all join in.

Nip a little nip,
tuck a little tuck,
dance in a circle,
you'll have good luck.

THE SKATER

By Lilian Moore

Wind in my hair
Wings at my heels

I'm sailing down-street
On whirring wheels.

I'm taking the curve
With a masterly swerve,

Gracefully speeding past
People who wait.

Surely they're saying,
"My, watch her skate!

She's fast! She's
Daring! The best of them all!"

How I hated to fall.

SPOOKY'S HALLOWEEN

By Natalie Savage Carlson • Illustrated by Andrew Glass

THE Bascombs had a black cat named Spooky. He had once belonged to the wicked witch who lived in the woods nearby. He had run away from her because he wanted to be a real pet instead of a witch's broom mate.

One night, the moon hung in the sky like a jack-o'-lantern. It was Halloween. The Bascomb children left in their costumes to play trick-or-treat. Their mother waited with a tray of goodies for those who would come to their door.

The third visitor was a boy in witch's costume. Instead of taking some of the goodies, he cried "Trick" and grabbed Spooky. Off they went to the witch's hut, where a great vulture was waiting by the door. "Look, Maw!" the boy said to the witch. "I played a trick and got a treat. Your old sidekick is my new pet. I'll take him to my playroom for the night and keep him there so he can't escape again."

The witch boy climbed on back of the vulture, with Spooky in front of him. He kicked the bird, and it spread its great wings for take-off. Higher and higher it flew, brushing the stars aside and creating a shadow on the moon.

To Spooky, flight on a vulture seemed even worse than on a broom. High over a muddy river, the vulture alighted at an aerie on a rocky ledge. The witch boy jumped off with the cat in his arms. Spooky could see there was no way down

except by a drop into the river. How could he escape? All night he lay awake thinking about it.

When morning came, the witch boy walked to the brink of the ledge. He breathed deeply of the fresh air. Sni-i-if, snu-u-uf!

Then Spooky had a sudden idea. He crept behind the witch boy, creepy-crawly, and suddenly yowled *"Yee-ow! Yee-ow!"*

The witch boy teeter-tottered for three seconds. Then he lost his balance and fell into the river.

Spooky jumped on the vulture and gave it a sharp slap with his paw. The bird flip-flapped off the ledge. Spooky could see the witch boy struggling ashore below.

The vulture's great wings swept through the clouds. But where was he taking Spooky? To another aerie high in the sky? To the witch's hut, where she would surely keep him?

Then Spooky found he could guide the bird by slapping it on this side or that side. He headed it for the Bascomb house. Suddenly the vulture spotted some of its kind gathered around a dead snake on the road below. It swept down and joined them for the feast.

Spooky jumped off and skedaddled down the road to the Bascomb house. He was glad Halloween was over.

WHAT'S BUGGING ME

By Jane Yolen

You know what bugs me?
Mosquitoes in the ear
Buzzing out a warning
That an itchy bite is near.

You know what bugs me?
A moth inside a tin
Of sugar after I just ate
Some sugar that was in.

You know what bugs me?
A cricket late at night
Who starts to sing just after
Mommy has turned out the light.

WISHING

By Beatrice Schenk de Regniers

I wish that I were six feet tall.
I wish I had a talking cat.
I don't have any cat at all,
And I am really rather small—
    The smallest in my class!

I wish that I could somehow fly.
I wish I were an acrobat.
But I don't think I'd ever try
To walk a tightrope way up high—
    I'm too scared . . . alas!

I know my wishes won't come true.
And what is more, the truth is that
I do not really want them to.

MORTIMER'S DREAM

By Ann McGovern • Illustrated by Neil Waldman

MORTIMER loved everything Indian. He loved Indian games and Indian songs. He had an Indian tepee in his room. He slept in it every night and played in it every day.

Mortimer had a friend named Joe who ran the grocery store down the street. Joe's real name was Quick Fox, but everyone called him Joe. Joe was a Sioux Indian. He often told Mortimer tales about Indians. Mortimer loved these story times with Joe.

One summer day Mortimer asked Joe, "How did you get the name Quick Fox?"

"When I was a boy," said Joe, "I was taken to a special place far from home. I was left alone in the woods for four days and four nights."

"All alone?" Mortimer's voice was full of fear. Mortimer hated the dark.

"Yes," said Joe, "and I couldn't have a bite to eat or drink for four days."

"Not even a cookie?" Mortimer asked.

"No, not a thing to eat," said Joe. "Every night I prayed to the Great Spirit to send me a special sign. It was supposed to come to me in a dream. On the last night, I dreamed of a fox running through the woods.

"By then I was very hungry and thirsty and weak in the knees. I was taken to a wise medicine man. I told him about the fox I saw in my dream. Then the medicine man knew what name to give me."

"Let's see if I get it," Mortimer said. "Your Indian name is Quick Fox. So your sign must be a fox!"

"Right," said Joe. "I became as swift as a fox too. I painted foxes on my tepee and on my shield, I made up songs and dances to my special fox spirit. And best of all, I knew my fox spirit would protect me from dangers all my life."

"I wish I had a spirit like that," said Mortimer.

WHEN Mortimer got home from visiting Joe, he crept into his tepee to think. His cat crept in with him.

He thought about how brave the Sioux Indians were. He wished that he, too, could be as brave as an Indian.

Mortimer thought of all the things he

was afraid of—thunder and lightning, darkness, strange places, and big barking dogs. He thought hard for about an hour. Then he went to see his mother.

"I'm not crazy about the name Mortimer," he said. "I've made up my mind to have an Indian name." He told his mother how Indian boys got their names.

"But I could never sleep out in the woods alone for four days and four nights. You wouldn't let me, would you?" Mortimer asked.

"Probably not," his mother said. "Four days and four nights are a long time for you to be without food or water. You would get very hungry and thirsty. And besides, we would miss you."

"I would miss you too," Mortimer said.

"But how about overnight in the woods in back of the house?" his mother said.

Mortimer knew every rock, every tree, and every cave in the woods in back of his house. He often played there in the daytime. But at night, he thought, the woods would be very dark and very scary.

"What do you say, Mortimer?" his mother asked.

"I'll do it," he said. "And I will have a dream that will give me a wonderful Indian name and a spirit to protect me from harm."

THAT afternoon before supper, Mortimer gathered together the things he might need: a flashlight and a pillow; a whistle to blow—just in case; a raincoat—just in case; his old blanket that made him feel good in bad times—just in case.

His mother said, "I'll pack you some fruit and cookies."

"No," said Mortimer. "If an Indian boy could go without food and water for four days, I can go without fruit and cookies for one night." But he had two helpings of chocolate ice cream at supper to make up for it.

At last he was ready for his big adventure.

"If it rains, we'll come and get you," his father said.

"No," said Mortimer. "That would spoil everything." Mortimer hugged his cat and kissed his mother and father good-bye.

"Be ready to stop calling me Mortimer," he told them. "I'll have another name in the morning."

Mortimer walked to the woods. He arranged his pillow and blanket for sleeping. He looked up at the sky.

"O Spirit, please send me a sign in my dream tonight," he begged. "And make it a good sign, please."

The sun set and the woods grew dark. Very dark and very strange and very scary.

Mortimer turned on his flashlight. The rocks and trees he knew by day did not look the same at night.

The wind moaned through the trees.

Branches swayed and creaked. An owl hooted. A wild thing howled in the night.

Mortimer thought of blowing his whistle. He thought of running home. It would only take him two minutes.

Then he thought of the dream he might have. He thought of exciting Indian names.

"O Mighty Spirit," he called. "Please send me a sign as fast as you can."

Just then there was a flash of lightning and a clap of thunder. Rain came pouring down.

Mortimer got so scared he dropped his flashlight. The flashlight went out.

There was darkness everywhere. Wet darkness everywhere. He was cold and wet and very scared.

"Hurry up, Spirit!" he called.

Just then Mortimer heard a new sound. Something was howling. Something was bounding through the woods toward him!

Was it a dog? A gang of robbers? Two big dogs? Without his flashlight, he could not see a thing.

Mortimer cried out, "You gotta send me a sign, O Spirit! Hurry!"

The howling got louder, Mortimer began to run. He ran right into something wet and furry!

"Go away, whoever you are!" he said in his loudest voice.

Whatever it was bounded away in the dark.

Now that the scary thing was gone, Mortimer breathed a shaky sigh. "It could have been a bear," he thought.

He put on his raincoat and a minute later the rain stopped.

Mortimer felt around in the dark for his flashlight. Maybe it would work now. But it still didn't.

Suddenly he tripped. A heavy branch fell on his leg. Mortimer leaned over and tugged and tugged at the branch. He tried again and again. At last he was able to move the heavy branch and free his leg. He rubbed his leg until it stopped hurting.

Then he tried to think about sleep.

"As soon as I fall asleep, I'll have my special dream," he said. "Then I'll know my Indian name."

But Mortimer was too scared to go to sleep. He began to think of ways to tire himself out. He hopped on one foot a hundred times. He lay down on his old blanket on a bed of soft wet pine needles. And sure enough, it wasn't long before he grew sleepy.

"Please, please, Mighty Spirit," he called softly into his pillow. "Please send me a dream. Please send me a good dream." Then Mortimer fell asleep.

The stars came out and the moon shone on Mortimer sleeping in the woods. He did not stir.

Mortimer did not dream of a strong wolf

or a swift eagle or a wise owl. He did not dream of a sharp-eyed hawk or a running deer.

When the sun rose, Mortimer woke up and tried to remember his dream. He couldn't remember dreaming a thing!

"No dream! I had no dream at all," Mortimer cried. He felt horrible.

He hurried home to drop off his things and ran straight to see his friend Joe.

"How was your special place?" Joe asked. "Did you get a name you like?"

Mortimer began to cry. "I didn't dream," he cried. "I didn't dream a single thing. Maybe it was because I only stayed out in the woods for one night. I should have stayed out four nights like you did. Then maybe I would have had a dream and a new name."

Joe handed Mortimer a handkerchief. "Tell me what happened," Joe said. "Tell me everything."

So Mortimer stopped crying and told him everything. He told him how the woods got dark and scary. He told him about the thunder and lightning and how the rain soaked him. He told him about his flashlight going out. He told him about scaring away the big furry thing that could have been a bear. He told him about the heavy branch that fell on his leg and how he got his leg out from under it.

Joe listened carefully. Then he said, "Mortimer, you are not an Indian, and I am not a medicine man. But this I know. Your spirit came to you."

"It did?" Mortimer asked. "How?"

"Your spirit is in yourself," Joe told him. "Your spirit is brave. It helped you stay all night in the dark woods with the wild creatures.

"Your spirit is strong. It helped you lift a heavy log off your leg.

"Your spirit is wise. It helped you figure out how to go to sleep. I would be proud to have a spirit like yours," Joe said.

"Would you really?" Mortimer felt a lot better. "But I think I still want an Indian name," he said.

"What Indian name do you think you should have?" Joe asked.

Mortimer was quiet for a moment.

"All I can think of is The-Boy-Who-Did-Not-Dream," Mortimer said.

"I like your name much better," said Joe.

On the way home, Mortimer thought about what Joe had told him.

When he got home, he ran to his room and painted a special sign for his tepee and his shield:

MORTIMER

Then he made up songs and dances to his own special Mortimer spirit.

"That's me, Mortimer," he said. "Mortimer the brave, Mortimer the strong, Mortimer the wise!"

Illustration by Rosemary Wells

YOUR BIRTHDAY CAKE

By Rosemary Wells

Your birthday cake is made of mud
Because I cannot cook.
I cannot read a recipe or follow in a book.
I'm not allowed to use the stove
To simmer, roast, or bake.
I have no money of my own to buy a birthday cake.
I'm sure to get in trouble if I mess around with dough.
But I've made your birthday cake of mud
Because I love you so.

BIRTHDAY SONG

By Patricia Hubbell

At last comes a morning
  when nothing is wrong—
When nothing is ragged,
  or tattered, or torn—
A lollipop morning
  all slick with sweet licks,
When clouds swim in rivers,
  bugs balance on sticks,
And even the turtles
  attempt some high kicks—
It's my birth happy morning,
My happy birth day,
My Hello-to-the-World,
My Happy Hooray!

SOAPY SMITH, THE BOASTFUL COWBOY

or The Skunk in the Bunkhouse

Written and illustrated by Glen Rounds

ONE Sunday afternoon on Rattlesnake Ranch, Soapy Smith and the other cowboys are sitting in the shade of the corral telling each other big windies about the places they've been and the fancy riding they've done one time and another.

Soapy is a great one for bragging and has just finished explaining how he was present in person the day Pecos Bill rode the cyclone down to nothing, when Hairpants Hagadorn points toward the bunkhouse and hollers, "Lookit th' little chore boy run!"

They all look to where Hairpants is pointing, and right enough the little chore boy seems to have a burr under his tail for sure. He's coming so fast, his shadow is ten feet behind, and at every jump he hollers, "Skunk in the bunkhouse! Skunk in the bunkhouse!"

"A skunk, eh?" says Soapy. "A striped kitty?"
"Sic the dog on it!" says Hairpants.
"Git the shotgun an' shoot it!" says Bug-eye.
"Naw, that'd mess th' place all up," says Highwater. "What yuh gotta do is smoke him out!"

"Now boys," says Soapy, "don't git all in a lather over a small matter like this. All yuh hafta do t' git a skunk out of th' house peaceful is t' pick him up by th' tail and carry him gentle-like, and he won't do a thing."

"I don't believe it'll work!" says Hairpants.
"As long as yuh hold him by th' tail he's safe!" says Soapy.
"A skunk's a skunk, no matter how yuh grab him, I say," says Bug-eye.
"I still say smoke him out!" says Highwater.

But Soapy steps inside the bunkhouse. "Boys," says he, "I've handled a sight of varmints in my time. Bears, panthers, bobcats, an' Gila monsters. I know all about 'em. You just stand back and watch close how I do it!"

Soapy eased over to where the skunk was hiding behind a box, and gently picked it up by the tail. "See how easy?" he says proudly as he carries the critter outside.

"Yeah!" says Hairpants. "But how in tarnation are you going to turn him loose?"

"Say!" says Soapy, "I hadn't thought of that!"
And for all anyone knows he may still be sitting there trying to figure a way to let go of that skunk!

YOU ARE

Words and Music by Tom Glazer
Illustrated by Karen Gundersheimer

Em   Am   Em   D   C   C *(Echo)*

1. Who's the most won - der - ful | kid here? | You are! | You are!

Em   Am   Em   D   C   D   *(Echo)*

Who's the most mar - vel - ous | kid here? | You are! | You are!

Em   D   Am   C   Am   C

Who is the sweet - est, nic - est, dear - est, smart - est, tast - i - est,

D   D⁷   Em   C *(Echo)*   Em   Em *(Echo)*

Repeat Ad lib.

most de - lic - ious? You are!__ You are!__ You are!__ You are!__

2) Who's the most scrumptious child here,
    You are! (echo: You are!)
  Who is the loveliest child here,
    You are! (echo: You are!)
  Who is fantastic, terrific, sensational, the
    yummiest, niftiest, spiffiest brat here,
    You are! (echo: You are!)

3) Who makes me glad every day I'm alive,
    You do! (echo: You do!)
  Who makes my heartbeats go flippety-flop,
    You do! (echo: You do!)
  Who makes the gloomiest day seem sunny,
  Who turns my saltiest tears to honey,
    You do! (echo: You do!)

4) Repeat first verse

Suggestions for performing the song:

The parent, teacher, or song leader can sing the song solo, with the children simply singing each echo, to repeat the words "You are" and "You do."

Or the song can easily be taught to the children line by line with one half of the group singing the echo section to each other back and forth. The children, I have found, find it fun to point to the song leader or the other singers on the words "You are" and "You do," making it a simple finger play.

As recorded by Tom Glazer on his LP/tape: *More Music for 1's & 2's (& 3's & 4's)* CMS Records, Mt. Vernon, N.Y. 16553

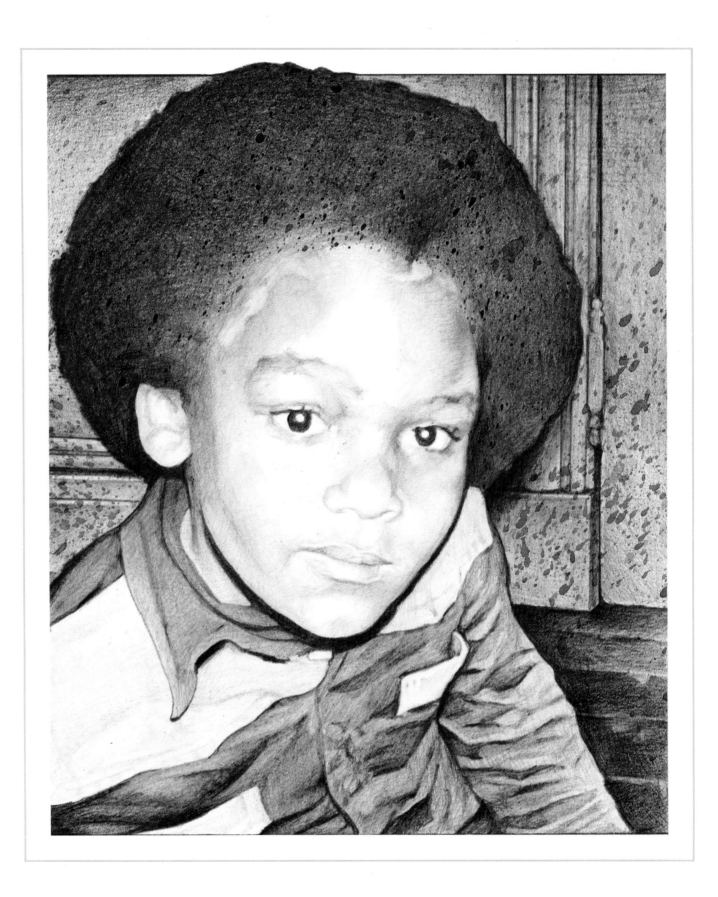

SHAWN AND UNCLE JOHN

Written and illustrated by John Steptoe

MY name is Shawn. I live with my mama and my grandma. My uncle John used to live with us, but I didn't know him too well. When he went away to school, I got his old room.

I like having my own room. I can do what I want there. I go there when I get angry or when I just want to think and not be bothered.

One day Grandma got a letter. She was very excited. "Shawn! Your uncle John is coming home!" she said.

"Yeah?"

"Yes, he's finished school. And he'll stay here until he goes to his new job."

"Where will he be sleeping, Grandma?"

"Well, Shawn, he'll only be here a few weeks. We'll talk about that later. Okay?"

I knew what that meant. It meant giving up my room to Uncle John and sleeping on the couch or somewhere. I didn't like that.

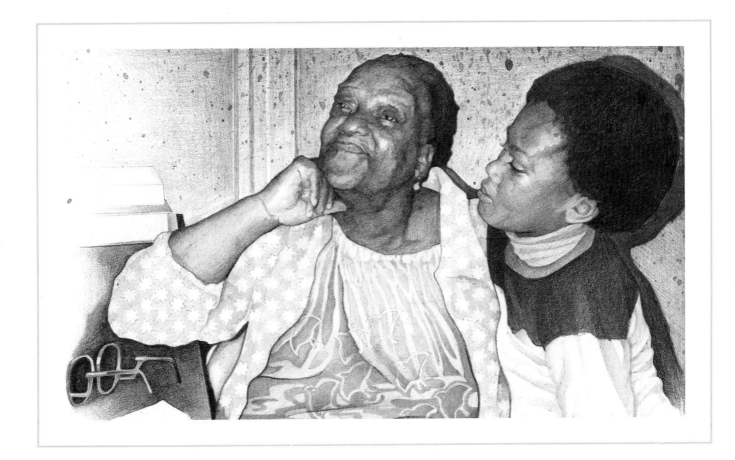

When he came, that's just what happened. I had to sleep on the couch.

He had a baldy-bean haircut, and he wore silly bow ties, and I had to sleep on the couch.

He took me to the movies and stuff, tryin' to be my friend.

But it didn't work 'cause I would never like him. He was a dummy. He stayed longer than a few weeks too. And I had to sleep on the couch.

One day I got home from school and he wasn't there. So I decided to go see what he'd been doin' in my room. I was told not to, but it *was* my room.

I knew Uncle John drew pictures of buildings, so I found a lot of them on his table. I knew I could draw better pictures than those. So I took one of his pens and opened one of his bottles of ink and . . . Oops! The ink went over everything.

Grandma was very angry with me.

Well! It was good for him anyway! I don't care if he spanks me! It was *my* room before he came.

Then Uncle John finally came home and saw the mess. He didn't even yell. He said what I did could be fixed. He even said he was sorry he'd taken my room, and he'd be gone by Monday.

Boy! And I thought he'd spank me for sure!

My real daddy died when I was a baby, and I s'pose it's not so bad havin' Uncle John around.

"Uncle John?"

"Yeah?"

"Are we goin' out this weekend like we always do?"

"Sure!"

"Could we do something before we go?"

"Sure, Shawn, what do you want to do?"

"I want you to take me to get a haircut just like yours."

"Okay!"

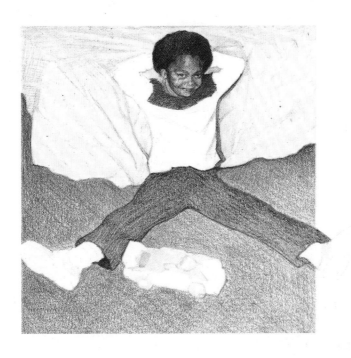

MY DOCTOR

Written and illustrated by Rosemary Wells

My doctor is so helpful
When I have a dismal day.
He decelerates my fever
And he sends my chills away.
He's wonderful with viruses
and idiopathic spots
But I wish he'd do it nicely
Without stinging, pinging,
Nicking, pricking,
Sharp and shocking shots.

HOW SPIDER LEARNED TO READ

Written and illustrated by Robert Kraus

IT'S BUG BOOK WEEK

I was feeling very sad.
It was Bug Book Week . . .
but I couldn't read!

1.

I went over to Ladybug's house.
Fly was there as usual reading
The Fly Paper.
"I can't read!" I said.

2.

"Reading is fun," said Ladybug.
She sat down and began to read
My Fair Ladybug.

"I wish I could read," I said.
"It's not hard," said Ladybug.
"Immerse yourself in books."
"Go soak your head," said Fly.

So I got in the bathtub with
a lot of books. But it didn't
help. I still couldn't read.

"Of course not," said Ladybug. "You have to hear someone read the words first."
"I don't get it," I said.
"Look at the page as I read," said Ladybug.

"I just listen and watch? Then I can read too?"

"Sure," said Ladybug. "You learn to read by listening and talking. And then by reading yourself."

"Hoorah!" I said. "Bring on those great Spider books. Now I can read!"

"Hummph!" said Fly and that is

TAKING CARE OF ROSIE

By Patricia Reilly Giff • Illustrated by Blanche Sims

O N Friday, my friend Anna marches up to the blackboard with her book.
She has to read aloud.
Miss Foster claps when Anna is finished. "Lovely," she says.
I duck down in my seat. My turn is next.
I don't even know which story to pick.
My hands are wet.
My mouth is dry.
I'll never be able to read in front of everyone.

Then the bell rings.
I take a deep breath.
I don't have to worry about school, or reading, for two whole days.
On the way home, Anna skips up and down the curb.
"Oh, Christine," she says. "I'm so glad it's over, and I made only two mistakes."
"You couldn't tell." I shake my head. "I'm probably going to make a hundred."
We wave at the corner.

"I think my mother's having our baby next week," Anna calls back. "I hope it's a girl. Just like your sister, Rosie."
I don't tell Anna that taking care of Rosie isn't so easy.

Rosie is three.
She has a fat belly, and gum in her hair, and sometimes, her pants are wet.

She makes lipstick Rosies on the hall wall with huge heads and spider arms
and legs,
and screams when someone tries to wash them off.

And did I say she wishes she could read?

Every morning, after breakfast, she runs around in my yellow boots,
and reads my book upside down. She likes the story about the train.
"Come back," I say. "Miss Foster hates it when I'm late."

But Rosie keeps going.
"The train goes up the hill," she says.
"Don't I sound like a train?
Listen, Christine.
Chuga. Chuga. Chuga."
When I get to school, three corn crispies
are stuck to my book.

This Friday, I drop my books on the table,
and call hello to my mother.
"What did you do with my Gummy
Bears?" I ask Rosie.
Rosie points down.
"Down in the basement?" I ask. "Down
there in the dark?"
Rosie shakes her head back and forth.
That means yes.

I wish I had those Gummy Bears.
I love the orange ones.
Rosie starts down the stairs.
"We'll get them now," she says.
"Follow my back."
But I'm not going down
in that basement.
Not me.
I sit on the top step and wait.
I can hear Rosie.
"The train has too much to pull,"
she says.
"Chuga shoom. Chuga shoom."

Then she stops talking.
"What are you doing?" I call down.
I know what she's doing.
"Mom," I yell. "Rosie's eating my candy."
But my mother's all the way upstairs.

"Rosie," I say. "Come on up here."
"Chuga shoom," she answers.
I look at the dark for a minute,
then I inch my way downstairs.
Rosie's sitting in the middle of the floor,
eating the heads off my Gummy Bears.
I look around.
It's really not so bad after all.
I reach into the bag for the last
orange bear.

On Saturday, I open my book.
Which story should I read to the class
on Monday?
"Watch out for Rosie," my mother calls
up to me.
Rosie puts on one shoe and plops last
winter's hat on her head.
"Hurry," she says. "We go backyard."
"I'm trying to read," I tell my mother.
"Be an angel," my mother says. "Read in
the yard."

Outside, we sit on the grass.
Rosie leans over my shoulder.
I can hear her breathing.
"Read me the train," she says,
"or maybe a cow."
"There aren't any cows," I say and stop.
A fat bee is buzzing over our heads.
"Yeow," I say. "Let's get out of here."
Rosie looks up. "Nice. Look."
After a minute, the bee zips away.
"I'll read the train," I say.

On Sunday morning, Rosie starts
to scream.

"Save me, somebody, I'm drowning."
I can hear the water sloshing in the sink.
My mother is washing her hair.
"Christine," Rosie yells. "Help. Bring a
book."

In the bathroom, Rosie is bent over
the sink.
She's holding a yellow washcloth over
her eyes.
"Chuga, chuga," I begin.
Rosie stops screaming. "Read loud,"
she says.
"Friendly. Like the story lady on TV."
I start over in my best voice.
My mother rinses out the soap and
wraps a towel around Rosie's head.
"Good, Christine." Rosie hops on
one foot.
"I love that chuga-chuga part," she says.

On Sunday night, I go into my mother's
bedroom.
She's wearing a skinny red dress
and nail polish.
"Are you going out?" I ask.
My mother fiddles with one earring.
"Yes."
"That means Mrs. Carr is coming."
My mother pats my cheek.
"I hate it when you go out," I say.
"It's lonesome,
and I can't get to sleep."

Later, I lie in bed, still as a stick,
and keep my eyes open forever.

I hear Rosie climbing out of her bed.
She sneaks in with me.
"Tell me the book," she whispers.
She puts her thumb in her mouth.
"Chuga, chuga."
I close my eyes and yawn.
"Chuga, chuga," I whisper too.
And then it's morning. . . .

Monday morning. It's my turn to read.
I go up to the front of the classroom
with my book.
I can hardly swallow.
Everyone is waiting.
I look at the empty seat in the back
of the room,
and make believe Rosie is sitting there.
She's wearing her old green hat
with the pom-pom,
and chewing on a Gummy Bear head.
I open the book to the train story
and begin.
"Read loud," Rosie would say.
"Read friendly."
I read slowly, and try to sound like
the train.
I look up when I finish.
Then Miss Foster smiles and claps.
So does the rest of the class.

Back in my seat, I lean over
toward Anna.
"Did the baby come yet?" I ask.
She shakes her head. "Not yet."
I cross my fingers. "I hope it's a girl,"
I say. "Just like Rosie."

TOAD'S TRICK
A Kanuri Fable

By Verna Aardema • Illustrated by Will Hillenbrand

ONE morning a toad said to a rat, "I can do something you can't do."

"What!" cried the rat. "You don't even know how to run. You just throw yourself, *lop*—and then you stop and look around."

Toad said, "See those men sitting under that ficus tree? I'll go right through them and not be harmed. If *you* can do that, I will eat my words." So *lop, lop, lop,* went Toad toward the men under the tree.

"Ah, there's a toad," said one of the men.

"Do not harm it," said another. "Toads eat bugs."

And the toad hopped between the stools of the men and returned to the rat by a different way.

Then the rat set out with great speed, *kipido, kipido, kipido,* straight for the group of men.

"A rat!" yelled one man. "Get him!"

In and out between the stools scrambled the rat. The men tried to step on him, they tried to stomp him with the legs of their stools. Then one man chased him off with a long stick, whacking him again and again! Finally the rat dove into a hole in the ground and was saved.

Later, when the rat returned to the toad, he said, "You were right. There is something you can do that I cannot."

And that is true for all of us—there are some things that only we can do.

WHEN I WAS A LITTLE BOY, I HAD THE SAME DREAM
OVER AND OVER AGAIN....I WOULD PUSH MY TONGUE
AGAINST THE ROOF OF MY MOUTH, CLOSE MY EYES
AND BEFORE I KNEW IT, I'D BE FLOATING AROUND IN
THE CLOUDS....

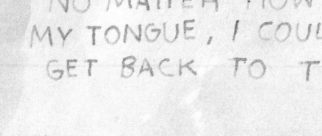

Illustration by Tomie dePaola

GOD'S BREAD
A Traditional Jewish Tale
Retold by Barbara Cohen
Illustrated by Patricia Polacco

THE holy city of S'fad nestles in the mountains of northern Israel. Famous rabbis, scholars, mystics, and saints have walked its steep, narrow streets for hundreds of years. Ordinary people, like you and me, have walked them too.

Two ordinary men named Meir and Yakov lived in S'fad a long, long time ago. Meir, a miller, was very rich. Yakov, the janitor at the synagogue, was very poor.

Meir was no scholar. To tell the truth, he wasn't even very smart. Because he worked hard all week, he had a lot of trouble staying awake during the long Sabbath morning service. But the hard wooden bench on which he dozed was uncomfortable. He'd wake up for a moment or two, rearrange himself, and fall back to sleep.

One Sabbath morning he awakened just long enough to hear the rabbi chant, "You shall take choice flour and bake of it twelve loaves. . . . Place them on the pure table before the Lord in two rows, six to a row."

Those words were part of the biblical reading for the week. But Meir didn't realize that. When the service was over, and he woke up for good, he thought God had spoken directly to him in a dream. "How wonderful," he said to his wife when he got home. "God chose an ordinary, not-very-smart man like me to speak to. But all he asked for was twelve loaves of bread."

"I didn't know that God ate bread," said Mrs. Meir.

"Who are we to question God?" Meir took twelve special twisted Sabbath loaves and rushed back to the synagogue. He placed the loaves on the table in front of the holy ark, covered them with the velvet cloth, and left.

A few moments later Yakov the janitor

arrived. "Oh, God," he cried, "what am I to do? How am I going to feed my wife and seven children? We spent the bit of money we had on a doctor for our sick baby. We have nothing to eat, and no way of buying anything. Surely, we will all die."

As the janitor spoke, he wandered about the room, straightening it up. When he came to the table in front of the ark, he saw that the cloth looked strangely lumpy. He lifted it, and discovered the twelve loaves in two rows, six and six. "Oh, God," he exclaimed, "thank you, thank you. I never expected my prayer to be answered so quickly! It's a miracle." He hurried home with his treasure as fast as he could.

Later, Meir said to his wife, "I'm going back to the synagogue. I want to find out if God ate my loaves." When he saw that the bread was gone, he exclaimed, "A miracle! God has accepted the humble offering of an ordinary, not-very-smart man like me."

The following Sabbath, Meir once again left twelve loaves underneath the cloth on the table in front of the ark. Later, Yakov, too, returned to the synagogue. "Oh, God," he cried, "I hate to be such a pest, but I'm in trouble again. We ate seven of the loaves you gave us, we sold four, and we gave one to charity, as you have decreed. Now we are destitute once more. I'm afraid we need another miracle if we're not to die of starvation." This time Yakov knew where to look. The cloth was lumpy; underneath were twelve loaves in two rows, six and six. Once again, he thanked God and carried the bread home.

Months passed, months and more months. Every Sabbath, Meir left twelve

loaves on the table. Every Sabbath, Yakov took them home. Meir was convinced God ate his bread. Yakov was convinced God gave him his bread.

One day the rabbi did not go home for lunch right after the service. In the anteroom, he was looking up the answer to a difficult question someone had asked him, when he heard a noise in the sanctuary. He poked his nose through the door and saw Meir place twelve loaves of Sabbath bread underneath the tablecloth. Meir left, and a few moments later, Yakov arrived. The rabbi watched while Yakov uncovered the bread and took it away with him.

"Now I understand," the rabbi said to himself. "I understand why a smile of satisfaction always seems to beam from Meir's face, even when he's sleeping through the service. And I understand why these days Yakov and all the little Yakovs look so plump and healthy."

The rabbi sent for Meir and Yakov. They came to see him in the synagogue. He told them what had happened. "Meir, the bread you offer on the table is eaten by Yakov. Yakov, the bread you eat is a gift from Meir."

"Oh," said Meir sadly, "and I thought all along I was giving it to God."

"Oh," said Yakov sadly, "and I thought all along I was getting it from God."

"But don't you see?" said the rabbi. "You were—both of you. When you give to those who need it, you are giving a gift to God. And when you accept from those who can afford it, you are receiving a gift from God. More than when you pray, more than when you study, it is then that God is truly with you."

THE CLIMB
A Modern-day Fable

By Patricia C. McKissack • Illustrated by Brian Pinkney

'DOJO was the oldest and wisest of the Kikuyu elders. His ears had heard many sounds, and his eyes had seen many sights. He was at peace with everything and everyone around him. It was said that W'Dojo could smell the rains long before they fell and that he could touch the soil and tell if it was time to plant. He was rarely wrong. Now W'Dojo had a feeling that he would soon die, and he was preparing for the event.

Among the young boys of the Kikuyu villages, it was a time for learning. This year they had a special honor. W'Dojo was to be their teacher.

Thirty boys sat quietly at their teacher's feet, eager to learn. They had been sent to learn as much of the teacher's wisdom as they could. When old W'Dojo spoke, he extended an invitation to each boy: "Those who want to learn, come follow me to the mountain. Begin at sunrise. Don't be afraid or worried, for the way will be clearly marked."

All the boys were eager to learn and chorused, "We will follow you to the mountain."

Early the next morning, twenty-five boys met on the road. Five boys had decided to sleep late and muttered, "Go on. We will catch up with you later." They never did.

By noon the sun was hot and the ground was dry and dusty. However, the path led to a water hole. The boys splashed and played in the fresh and cooling water. Five of the boys decided they would stay longer to play and have fun. "Go on. We will join you later," they said. Of course, they never did. Now only twenty boys traveled toward the mountain.

The day was long, and the way became narrow and difficult. Rocks blocked the path, and thornbushes scratched the boys' legs. "We are tired, and our feet are sore," five of the boys complained. "We must stop. You go on, and we will join you later." But that evening there were only fifteen boys left.

The path led to a deep, wide river. Crocodiles, looking like sleeping logs, lined its banks. Several of the boys were terribly frightened and turned back. Only seven boys followed the path past the crocodiles to shallow water, where they crossed in safety.

It was almost sunset. The boys were tired and hungry. They hadn't eaten all day. Suddenly the African plains came alive with the sounds of wild animals. Several of the boys cried out: "We have no fire!" "We have no food!" "We have no spears!" "We have nothing!" Four of them

hurried to a nearby village to wait until morning. When they returned the next day, they couldn't find the path that led to the mountain. So they returned to their homes.

The three boys who had stayed on the path slept in the trees and ate wild berries. They reached the foot of the mountain the next day at midmorning.

The mountain was huge, dark, and cold. The rocks were sharp and ragged. "I am afraid to climb," said one of the boys, and he turned back.

Just before they reached the top, the last two boys came to a deep cleft in the rocks. One jumped across without any trouble. The other stood looking into the deep, dark split. "I can't jump," he said. "I can't."

"It looks hard," cried the first boy, "but try. If old W'Dojo could jump across, you can too. He told us not to be afraid. Try."

The second boy stood looking at the split in the rock. "No," he said. "Learning is not worth this much." He turned and walked away.

The last boy climbed until he came to a cave in the side of the mountain. W'Dojo sat at the entrance, waiting.

"Welcome, my brother," the old one said. "You truly want to learn. And so it shall be. You are worthy of what I have to give. What is your name?"

The boy answered, "I am Jomo."

"Come, Jomo," said W'Dojo. "You have much to learn."

ORION, THE GREAT HUNTER

By Franklyn M. Branley

IN winter, the stars of the great hunter are in the sky. You can see them.

At about 9:00 P.M., look toward the south for three stars in a straight line. Above the three are two bright stars. And there are two bright stars below the line of three.

They are the main stars in Orion, the hunter. The three stars in a line are Orion's belt. The two stars above the belt are Orion's shoulders. And the two stars below the belt are his knees.

The shoulder stars are Betelgeuse and Bellatrix. Look carefully and you'll see that Betelgeuse (that's *bay' tel jus*) is a red star.

The knee stars are Saiph and Rigel.

The belt stars are Alnitak, Alnilam, and Mintaka.

The names of all these stars are strange. You have probably never heard them before. They are Arabic words. They are from a different language, and that's why they sound strange. Now you know some Arabic words.

When you look at Orion you will see rather dim stars curving out from Betelgeuse. These make the right arm of the hunter. He carries a big club.

You will also see stars curving out from Bellatrix. They make the hunter's left arm. In it he carries a shield made from a lion's skin.

In Greek legend Orion was the most powerful of all hunters. He fell in love with a girl whose father was the king of a Greek island. As it happened, there were a lot of wild animals on the island. Orion hunted them and rid the island of the animals.

Orion wanted to marry Merope, the king's daughter. But the king thought she could find another person for her husband. Orion tried to get the king's consent, but the king would not change his mind.

Orion decided he would take Merope, and the two escaped from the island.

When the king heard about the escape, he called in Artemis, who was an important Greek goddess. She hunted down Orion and shot him with an arrow. After she shot Orion, Artemis placed him among the stars, where he has remained ever since.

Merope survived and later was forced to marry someone else.

As you look at Orion on a winter's night you might think about this story. Also, see if you can name the stars—or some of them.

Remember, notice that Betelgeuse is a red star. It is a supergiant star. Our sun is about a million miles across. The diameter of Betelgeuse is 500 million miles. It seems small because it is so far away. Light takes 527 years to travel to us from Betelgeuse. Sunlight takes only about eight minutes to travel to us from the sun, our nearest star.

If you look carefully at Rigel you will see that it is a blue-white star. It is 23,000 times brighter than the sun. But it is much farther away than the sun. Light leaving Rigel today will get here 900 years from now—sometime in the twenty-ninth century.

Orion is still hunting. He is chasing Taurus, the bull. Running behind him are his two hunting dogs. One is called Canis Major—the big dog. The other one is Canis Minor, the little dog.

In winter, when the sky is dark and clear, go outside. Face south, and you'll find Orion. You'll also find Taurus and the hunting dogs.

I think you will agree that Orion is truly the great hunter of the sky.

THE MAGNIFICENT VOYAGER

By Seymour Simon

VOYAGER 2 was launched into space on August 20, 1977. It was the beginning of a lengthy photographic and scientific tour of the outer planets. Twelve years later, on August 25, 1989, after a fantastic journey of 2.8 billion miles, Voyager 2 whizzed past the blue storm clouds of Neptune. By all odds, the one-ton, ten-foot-tall space probe never should have made it that far and lasted that long.

Voyager 2 was supposed to have energy to last for only five years and to visit only two planets: Jupiter and Saturn. Just six months after launch, the primary radio receiver aboard Voyager 2 failed. The mission appeared to be doomed. But despite problems, the backup radio system went

Photo of Saturn taken by Voyager 1 on October 18, 1980.

NASA photo

into operation and the journey continued.

Voyager 2 swung past Jupiter in July, 1979, two years after launch. It took photographs of the changing cloud tops that cover the giant planet. It took close-up views of the turbulent Great Red Spot and other storms sweeping across the surface. It measured the ring around Jupiter and discovered a fainter, second ring. Voyager 2 also took many photographs of Jupiter's moons, from the exploding volcanoes on Io, to the billiard-ball smoothness of Europa, the lines on icy Ganymede, and the craters on Callisto.

Despite radiation damage to its instruments suffered near Jupiter, Voyager 2 continued on its journey. In August, 1981, it made its closest approach to Saturn—and developed another on-board problem. The platform that held the scientific instruments was stuck in the same position and couldn't be moved. Undaunted, the space engineers back on Earth figured out a way to shift the entire spaceship around to point the camera so that photographs could be taken. This maneuver used up more of the precious fuel that the space probe needed for continuing its mission.

NASA photo

Photo of the southern hemisphere of Jupiter and Io, its innermost Galilean satellite, taken by Voyager 2 on June 25, 1979. Io is the size of our moon.

But after a while, the platform began to move again and to be under control by the on-board computer.

By now, Voyager 2 was nearly out of fuel. So the space engineers figured out a new path, powered down the spaceship to save energy, and hoped for the best. The best was yet to be.

In January 1986, more than four years after it had photographed Saturn and eight and a half years after its launch from Earth, Voyager 2 swung around Uranus. Voyager photographed the blue-green clouds of Uranus and the five large moons that circle the planet. Voyager discovered that the planet's strange wobbling magnetic field had a long, curving tail that twisted and turned as the planet moved. Voyager also discovered that Uranus is lying on its side in space, with its south pole sometimes pointing at the sun and at other times its north pole pointing at the sun.

Three and a half more years passed, and Voyager 2 arrived at Neptune in the summer of 1989. By now, Voyager's video cameras were half blind, its aging electronics working at only one fifth their original speed, and its radio transmitter operating at the feeble power of a twenty-watt bulb. By the time the radio signal reached Earth, it had faded to less than ten quadrillionths of a watt. In addition, Neptune was lit by the distant sun only one thousandth as brightly as was Earth.

Despite all these obstacles, the super-computers developed on Earth since the Voyager launch did their job. Within minutes after receiving Voyager 2's weak signal, the photographs were made available for viewing by a wide television audience all over the world. Voyager 2 succeeded in sending back sharp photographs of stormy blue Neptune, its white fleecy clouds, its Great Dark Spot, and its rings. It also took close-up views of Neptune's largest moon, Triton, with its icy surface and bright ice cap.

By now Voyager 2 is on its way out of the solar system and into interstellar space. It is no longer able to transmit any signal. Its batteries are dead and its instruments are no longer working. But despite speeding silently along, the space probe still carries a message from Earth.

Aboard Voyager 2 is a greeting to the universe. It is a gold-plated phonograph record containing sounds of life on Earth, including the sound of thunder, the songs of birds and whales, human laughter, and musical selections that range from Bach's Brandenburg Concerto Number Two to Chuck Berry's "Johnny B. Goode." There are also messages in fifty-six Earth languages along with a list of instructions that scientists hope will give any space-faring aliens enough information for them to play the record.

Voyager 2 may still have many miles to go on its magnificent journey.

Dear friend,

This note is just to say
i wont be coming out to play.
Instead, I plan to find a space
and make myself a special place

where I can sit and read and go
to Africa or Mexico
or to the moon or anywhere
i can imagine. If you care

to join me come along, we'll see
how fundamental fun can be
for two or ten or even one.

> —your old friend,
> Everett Anderson

—Lucille Clifton

RAIN AND SNOW

By Lillian Morrison

The rain comes down in stripes
And hits the ground in dots
And wets the streets and houses
And all the empty lots.

The snow comes down like feathers
Drifting through the sky
And lightly lays a blanket
On roads and passersby.

A BRIDGE TO REMEMBER

Photo and text by Ken Robbins

THE Queensboro Bridge in New York City is both grand and beautiful. Made of steel girders fastened in strong crisscross shapes called trusses, it is 7,449 feet long. That is longer than twenty-four football fields put together.

Each morning at rush hour, thousands of cars and buses bring workers and shoppers and tourists over this bridge to cross the East River to Manhattan. Trucks carry heavy loads of everything from everywhere across the Queensboro Bridge and into the city. Much that is made or sold in the city goes out by truck across the bridge.

And every night, as the sun sets, the lights of the bridge and the lights of the city come on. Cars and buses stream across the bridge to take those tired workers and tourists back to their homes again.

TELL ME AGAIN!

By Else Holmelund Minarik

"TELL me again how you learned to ride a horse," I would ask my father when I was a little girl in Denmark. I was no more than four years old—too little to learn to ride a horse by myself. But I liked to hear my father tell his story.

And then he would begin.

"When I was a little boy, as little as you are now," he would say, "I wanted to ride the horses. But I was too small to mount a horse. So I would slip into my father's stables to be with the horses and admire them. Such big, powerful animals they were!

"The gentle workhorses stood quietly in their stalls, eating their hay. I would clamber up the side of one of the stalls and slide over onto the horse's back.

"Then I would clutch its mane and fancy us galloping over the meadows, down to the shore, and even into the sea.

"When I grew tall enough to mount a horse," he said, "my wish came true."

"You swim with the horses now," I said. "You even swim with Fiery. And he has spirit!"

Everybody knew about Fiery, the great black stallion with the fiery temper, and how he behaved when he first came to the stables. He reared in his stall. He snorted and kicked. He rolled his eyes. And everyone was afraid of him. Everyone, except my father.

I wanted to hear more. "Now tell how you made Fiery your friend," I begged. This was my favorite story.

"Well, little Else," my father went on, "I just talked to him. I talked as a friend. You must talk to a horse like Fiery.

"I'd say, 'No, little horse. No, my friend. You can't run free. You must learn to let me ride you.'

"And soon Fiery began to listen. He knew from my voice that I would be his friend."

So Fiery let my father teach him to carry a rider. Then Fiery would take my father across the soft green meadows or even into the lively waters of the northern sea.

I loved to see Father riding Fiery bareback into the sea. There they swam, Father and Fiery, out in the cold clear water.

Often I would watch them from the shore, holding tight to my mother's hand. They swam so bravely. I was so proud of them!

Then Father and Fiery would come splashing out of the water and gallop along the shore toward us. They made a fine stop—just in time!

Fiery towered over us. He tossed his head and shook a spray of sea water from his glistening black coat.

Father was laughing and patting Fiery's neck.

And I was making a wish.

I wished that someday I could have a horse, too . . . but a smaller one!

Father and Fiery in Denmark many years ago.

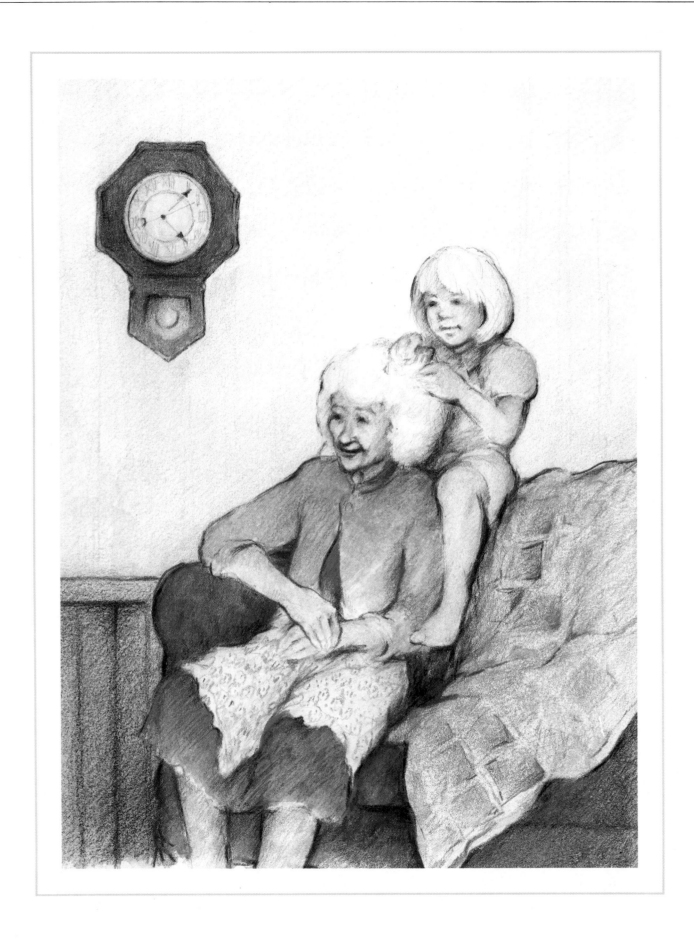

MY GRANDMOTHER'S HAIR

By Cynthia Rylant • Illustrated by Deborah Kogan Ray

WHEN I was living in my grandparents' small white house in Cool Ridge, West Virginia, I loved to comb my grandmother's hair. I was a thin, blondheaded little girl, and I would climb up on the back of the couch where my grandmother was sitting, straddle her shoulders with my skinny six-year-old legs, and I would gently, most carefully, lift a lock of her soft gray hair and make my little pink comb slide through it. This always quieted us both, slowed down our heartbeats, and we would sigh together and then I would lift up another lock.

We talked of many things as I combed her fine hair. Our talk was quiet, and it had to do with those things we both knew about: cats, baking-powder biscuits, Sunday school class. Mrs. Epperly's big bull. Cherry picking. The striped red dress Aunt Violet sent me.

But we didn't always talk. Sometimes we were quiet. We would just think, and my small hands would move in my grandmother's hair, twirling, curling, rolling that soft grayness around. We thought about good things, the big clock in the living room ticking, and sometimes my grandmother would shiver and we laughed.

I often put bobby pins in her hair, made pin curls with them, and the rest of the morning or afternoon my grandmother would wear these pin curls I had made. Later, I'd watch as she stood before her mirror, taking them out one by one, and her gray locks would be tight as bedsprings and would dance if you pulled on them. But when she brushed through these tight little wads of curl, her hair became magic and grew and covered her face like a lion's mane.

I thought many times that I might grow up to be a hairdresser, twirling ladies' gray locks into magic curls and watching their faces light up as they saw themselves change.

But I became a writer instead. And used my pen like a little pink comb, and got quiet, and thought good thoughts, and twirled and curled and rolled words into good stories. The stories became books, and with the same hands I had once combed her hair with, I handed these books to my grandmother and watched as she turned the pages one by one, the big clock in the living room ticking.

Sometimes she shivered and we laughed.

There are many ways to learn to be a writer.

THE LITTLE DOLL

By Charlotte Zolotow

I belong to a little girl
who makes me real
when she holds me
and rocks me
and says,
"You are beautiful
and my true friend
and I love you."

But alone in this chair
I am not real
I can only stay here
waiting.

Illustration by Taro Yashima

メキシコ椅子のうえのこけし
1976 芳雄

CONTRIBUTORS

VERNA AARDEMA has retold many African folktales. Among her books are *Bringing the Rain to Kapiti Plain* (a cumulative tale), *Oh, Kojo! How Could You!* and *Why Mosquitoes Buzz in People's Ears*, illustrated by Leo and Diane Dillon, which won the Caldecott Medal in 1976. She lives in Florida.

ALIKI has written and illustrated many picture books and has collaborated on others with her husband, Fritz Brandenberg. Her books range from "Let's-Read-and-Find-Out" books on dinosaurs and mammoths, to *A Medieval Feast*, with art suggesting tapestries of the Middle Ages. The Brandenbergs live in London.

JOHN ARCHAMBAULT—poet, journalist, and storyteller—has co-authored several books with Bill Martin Jr., including *Barn Dance!* and *The Ghost-Eye Tree*. Mr. Archambault lives in California.

FRANKLYN M. BRANLEY, astronomer emeritus and former chairman of the American Museum–Hayden Planetarium, is the author of numerous popular books for young people about astronomy and other sciences. He lives on Long Island, New York.

NATALIE SAVAGE CARLSON has traveled extensively and now lives in Rhode Island. Her years in Paris provided the background for books about the "Orphelines" and *The Family Under the Bridge*, a Newbery Honor Book. In 1966 she was the U.S. nominee for the International Hans Christian Andersen Award.

LUCILLE CLIFTON was named the 1969 Discovery Winner at the YMHA Poetry Center in New York City. The next year she entered the children's field with *Some of the Days of Everett Anderson*, the first of a poetic series about an engaging little city boy. She teaches at the University of California in Santa Cruz.

BARBARA COHEN, a recipient of the Sydney Taylor Award, has published twenty-five books for children and young adults, including *The Carp in the Bathtub*, illustrated by Joan Halpern, *Molly's Pilgrim*, illustrated by Michael Deraney, and *Canterbury Tales*, illustrated by Trina Schart Hyman. She lives in New Jersey.

TOMIE DEPAOLA has published more than one hundred books for children, for which he has won many honors, including the 1981 Kerlan Award from the University of Minnesota for "singular attainment in the creation of children's literature." In 1989 he was the U.S. nominee for the Hans Christian Andersen Award for Illustration. He lives in New Hampshire.

BEATRICE SCHENK DE REGNIERS, who lives in New York City, has had a varied career as a teacher, dancer, editor of children's books, and children's poet. Her book *May I Bring a Friend?*, illustrated by Beni Montresor, won the Caldecott Medal in 1965.

AILEEN FISHER lived for many years on a ranch in the Flagstaff Mountains of Colorado. Her poetry tells of her closest neighbors—rabbits, badgers, squirrels, raccoons, and more. In 1978 she won the second National Council of Teachers of English Award for Excellence in Poetry for Children. She is now living in Boulder, Colorado.

PATRICIA REILLY GIFF, a former teacher and reading consultant, has drawn from her classroom experience in a parade of books for children, which includes the "Polk Street" series. She lives in Fairfield County, Connecticut, where her family recently opened a bookstore for children.

ANDREW GLASS has illustrated many children's books, including several of the "Spooky" stories by Natalie Savage Carlson.

Many of his feelings about painting are revealed in the picture book that he also wrote called *Jackson Makes His Move*. Mr. Glass lives in New York City.

TOM GLAZER, one of the country's foremost balladeers, is also a successful songwriter and composer. For children he has compiled a number of song collections, among them: *Eye Winker, Tom Tinker, Chin Chopper: Fifty Musical Fingerplays* and *Tom Glazer's Treasury of Children's Songs*. He lives in Westchester County, New York.

KAREN GUNDERSHEIMER has written and illustrated a number of lively picture books for the very young, including *ABC Say with Me, One Two Three Play with Me,* and *Happy Winter,* and has contributed artwork to many other books. She and her husband live in Washington, D.C.

WILL HILLENBRAND drew on the basement walls of his family home before going on to art school in Cincinnati, where he lives today. He has received awards from the Society of Illustrators, the Society of Publishing Designers, and *Advertising Age*. Most recently he illustrated *Traveling to Tondo*, by Verna Aardema.

LILLIAN HOBAN, author and illustrator of the popular "Arthur the Chimp" stories, also illustrated many other books, among them the "First Grade" series, with Miriam Cohen, and several books about a delightful young badger named Frances, written by Russell Hoban. She lives in western Connecticut.

MARY ANN HOBERMAN has written sixteen books for young children, including *The Cozy Book* and *A House Is a House for Me*, collections of poems, and *Mr. and Mrs. Muddle*, a picture book illustrated by Catharine O'Neill. She lives in Greenwich, Connecticut.

NONNY HOGROGIAN has twice won the Caldecott Medal for her illustrations: for *Always Room for One More* (1966), written by Sorche Nic Leodhas, and for *One Fine Day* (1972), which she herself wrote. She and her husband, David Kherdian, live in Charlottesville, Virginia.

PATRICIA HUBBELL has lived all her life in the small town of Easton, Connecticut. She has been a newspaper reporter, prizewinning horsewoman, and gardener. Her most recent book of poetry for children is entitled *The Tigers Brought Pink Lemonade*.

DAVID KHERDIAN, poet, editor, teacher, and onetime publisher, is married to illustrator Nonny Hogrogian. His book *The Road from Home*, which tells the story of his mother's survival of the Turkish extermination of the Armenians during World War One, was a Newbery Honor Book and won the *Boston Globe–Horn Book* Award.

ROBERT KRAUS lives in New York City, where he was on the staff of *The New Yorker* for fifteen years. He then entered the juvenile-book field as an editor as well as an author-illustrator. Among his books are the "Spider" series and *Whose Mouse Are You?*, which is illustrated by José Aruego.

KARLA KUSKIN, winner of the 1979 National Council of Teachers of English Award for Excellence in Poetry for Children, has written many books for children—both poetry and prose—some with her own illustrations. Her cat, known formally as Toots, often sits by while she works. She lives in Brooklyn.

MADELEINE L'ENGLE is a prolific and highly acclaimed writer of books for adults as well as children. She is probably best known in the juvenile world for her trilogy of space-and-time fantasies: *A Wrinkle in Time*, *A Wind in the Door*, and *A Swiftly Moving Planet*. *A Wrinkle in Time* won the Newbery Medal in 1963. She lives in Connecticut and New York City.

EMILY ARNOLD McCULLY lives in New York City. She has illustrated many books, and created two series. One, of wordless books about a mouse family, includes *Picnic*, winner of the Christopher Award. Another series, with words, is about a bear family of actors. The most recent title is *Speak Up, Blanche*.

ANN McGOVERN, editor, poet, biographer, and storyteller, lives in New York State. She lists her hobbies as travel, scuba diving, and archeology. All show up in her books for children, which include *Too Much Noise*, illustrated by Simms Taback, and *Down Under, Down Under*, with photographs by Jim and Martin Scheiner.

PATRICIA C. McKISSACK has written a number of books for children. *Mirandy and Brother Wind*, illustrated by Jerry Pinkney, was a Caldecott Honor Book. She and her husband,

Frederick, who live in St. Louis, have co-authored eight books, including *The Long Hard Journey: The Story of the Pullman Car Porters*, winner of the Coretta Scott King Award.

BILL MARTIN Jr., teacher, lecturer, storyteller, singer, and guitar player, has become one of the outstanding writers in the field of education. His books for children include stories, poetry, and songs. He lives in New York City.

PETRA MATHERS was born in the Black Forest of West Germany and now lives in Portland, Oregon. Her droll and distinctive artwork has been widely exhibited. She has illustrated several children's books, among them *I'm Flying*, by Alan Wade, and her own books, *Maria Theresa* and *Theodor and Mr. Balbini*.

EVE MERRIAM has written more than fifty books for adults and children, and is an Obie-winning playwright. She received the 1981 Award for Excellence in Poetry for Children, given by the National Council of Teachers of English. She lives in New York City.

ELSE HOLMELUND MINARIK came into the children's book world with *Little Bear*, published in 1957 as one of the first "I Can Read" books. It was illustrated by Maurice Sendak, and became an instant favorite. In *To Ride a Butterfly* she gives a glimpse of her early childhood in Denmark. Today she lives in New Hampshire.

LILIAN MOORE, who lives in upper New York State, is a former teacher and director of the Arrow Book Club. She has written many books for children, both stories and poetry. She was the 1985 winner of the Award for Excellence in Poetry given by the National Council of Teachers of English.

LILLIAN MORRISON lives in New York City. Her many books of poetry include *The Sidewalk Racer* and *The Break Dance Kids* as well as two anthologies, *Sprints and Distances*, a collection of sports poetry, and *Rhythm Road, Poems to Move To*. She has also compiled six collections of folk rhymes, among them *Yours Till Niagara Falls* and *Best Wishes, Amen*.

BRIAN PINKNEY lives in New York City. He launched his career in the juvenile field with illustrations for *The Boy and the Ghost*, by Robert D. San Souci, *Harriet Tubman*, by Polly Carter, and *The Ballad of Belle Dorcas*, by William H. Hooks. His father is the noted artist Jerry Pinkney.

PATRICIA POLACCO lives in Oakland, California. In addition to writing and illustrating books she sculpts and paints eggs in the Ukrainian tradition. She received the International Reading Association Award for Young Readers for *Rechenka's Eggs*, and the Sydney Taylor Award for *The Keeping Quilt*.

DEBORAH KOGAN RAY lives in Philadelphia. She is a painter and illustrator whose work has received many awards and citations. Her most recent books include *hist whist* and *Little Tree*, both poems by e.e. cummings, and *Other Bells for Us to Ring*, by Robert Cormier.

KEN ROBBINS is a photographer and writer whose children's books include *Tools,* selected as one of the Best Illustrated Children's Books of 1983 by *The New York Times,* and *City-Country.* His photographs are widely exhibited on Long Island as well as in New York City. He lives in Easthampton, New York, with his wife, the writer Maria Polushkin.

ANNE ROCKWELL has written and illustrated innumerable books for young readers, including several board books highlighting activities and objects of a child's world (*At Night, In the Morning,* and *At the Playground)* and picture books. Several of her books have been honored by the American Institute of Graphic Arts. She lives in Connecticut.

GLEN ROUNDS was born in the Badlands of South Dakota and spent much of his life in the West as "a mule skinner, logger, carnival talker, sign painter, and lightning artist." His career as an author-illustrator began with publication of *Ol' Paul: The Mighty Logger* in 1949. Today he lives on Little Fiery Gizzard Creek near Southern Pines, North Carolina.

CYNTHIA RYLANT grew up in West Virginia, where she lived with her grandparents until she was eight. Her first book was *When I Was Young in the Mountains,* illustrated by Diane Goode, which was a Caldecott Honor Book, as was *The Relatives Came,* illustrated by Stephen Gammell. She lives in Ohio.

SEYMOUR SIMON has written more than a hundred science books for young readers. They include *The Paper Airplane Book* and *Pets*

in a Jar, as well as a series about sixth-grader Einstein Anderson, who solves any mystery or unravels any puzzle by applying sound principles of science. He lives on Long Island, New York.

BLANCHE SIMS is the illustrator of Patricia Reilly Giff's series on the Polk Street School, among other books. Recently, she illustrated *This Year I Took My Frog to the Library,* by Eric A. Kimmell, and nonfiction titles for Twenty-First Century Books. She lives in Westport, Connecticut.

PETER SPIER, a native of Holland, now lives in Connecticut. He won the Caldecott Medal in 1978 for *Noah's Ark,* a wordless picture book showing the growing animal population on the Ark. His many books feature panoramic watercolor paintings full of intriguing detail.

ROBIN SPOWART has illustrated a number of memorable picture books, including *A Rose, a Bridge, and a Wild Black Horse,* by Charlotte Zolotow, and *Songs from Mother Goose,* compiled by Nancy Larrick. Mr. Spowart lives in California.

JOHN STEPTOE published his first book, *Stevie,* when he was eighteen. It was hailed as "rare and beautiful." He went on to illustrate fifteen more books, nine of which he wrote. *Mufaro's Beautiful Daughters* was a Caldecott Honor Book, and won the *Boston Globe–Horn Book* Award as well as the Coretta Scott King Award. *The Story of Jumping Mouse* was also a Caldecott Honor Book, and *Mother Crocodile,* written by Rosa Guy, won the Coretta Scott King Award. He died in 1989, at the age of thirty-eight. The manuscript and paintings for "Shawn and Uncle John" were found among his papers by his literary executor, who gave permission for their use in *To Ride a Butterfly*.

TOMI UNGERER, born in Strasbourg, France, came to the United States in 1956 and began his career as a writer-illustrator of books for children. A long list of titles has earned him popularity and praise in America, England, Europe, and Japan. His books include *Zeralda's Ogre, No Kiss for Mother,* and *Moon Man.* He lives on a farm in West Cork, Ireland.

NEIL WALDMAN, who lives in White Plains, New York, is known for his jacket art as well as for illustrating picture books. His most recent title is a full-color version of the poem *The Highwayman.* He also creates postage stamps for Ghana, Sierra Leone, the Marshall Islands, and several other countries.

JOHN WALLNER lives in upstate New York. He has illustrated numerous books for children, among them the Christmas carol *Good King Wenceslas, The Boy Who Ate The Moon,* by Christopher King, and *When the Dark Comes Dancing,* a collection of poems compiled by Nancy Larrick.

ROSEMARY WELLS has published thirty-two books, including the "Max" board books and picture books. *Shy Charles* won the *Boston Globe–Horn Book* Award, and *When No One Was Looking,* a novel, won the Edgar Award for Juvenile Fiction from the Mystery Writers of America. She lives in Westchester County, New York.

NANCY WILLARD writes poetry, short stories, and novels for children as well as for adults. *A Visit to William Blake's Inn,* illustrated by Alice and Martin Provensen, won the first Newbery Medal given for a book of poetry, and was also a Caldecott Honor Book. She is a professor of English at Vassar College.

TARO YASHIMA was born on an island far to the south of Japan. His busy, peaceful village provides the background for several of his best-loved books, published after his move to the United States: *Plenty to Watch* (written with his wife, Mitsu), *The Village Tree,* and *Crow Boy* (1955). He lives in California.

JANE YOLEN's books for children include poetry, picture books, biographies, novels for young adults, and original fantasies. *Owl Moon,* illustrated by John Schoenherr, won the Caldecott Medal. She is also the editor of Jane Yolen Books at Harcourt Brace Jovanovich. She and her husband live in western Massachusetts.

CHARLOTTE ZOLOTOW, publisher emeritus of HarperCollins Junior Books, is the author of more than seventy picture books, among them *William's Doll* and *Mr. Rabbit and the Lovely Present.* She recently retired as the head of Charlotte Zolotow Books. In 1986 she received the Kerlan Award from the University of Minnesota, for "singular attainments in the creation of children's literature." She lives in Westchester County, New York.

AUTHOR, ARTIST, TITLE INDEX